A Merry Widow

Rae Shirley

A Samuel French Acting Edition

SAMUEL FRENCH

FOUNDED 1830

SAMUELFRENCH.COM
SAMUELFRENCH-LONDON.CO.UK

MERRY REGIMENT OF WOMEN

A One-Act Comedy

For Six Women and Three Men

CHARACTERS

Characters all but lately from the casts of one William Shakespeare:

JULIET'S NURSE

JULIET

DESDEMONA

LADY MACBETH

CLEOPATRA

KATE THE SHREW

HENRY V

ROMEO

PETRUCHIO

TIME: Whenever.

PLACE: Some fragment from the old Globe Theater.

3

MERRY REGIMENT OF WOMEN

SCENE: If possible, the stage is set on two levels. There are steps up center to platform. A small refectory table right center, set with 5 places, with quills, inkwells, sheets of paper, and place-cards indicating where each character will sit. If possible, right center, and apparently hanging from ceiling, a wooden, single-tier chandelier.

A stool down right. A throne type of chair on the opposite side of stage to the table. On this, JULIET'S NURSE is seated when the curtain goes up, gently snoring.

Music appropriate for the Elizabethan period may be played before, at rise, and at the close of the play.

AT RISE OF CURTAIN: JULIET'S NURSE is asleep in the chair L. She comes to with a start, and is agitated to find no sign of her charge.

NURSE. Juliet! Juliet! St, st! Where is the maid? 'Faith, not yet fourteen, and a right merry dance she leads me! Juliet! *[Shouting]* Jul - i - et!
JULIET'S VOICE. *[Off]* Romeo! Romeo!
                              Wherefore Art Thou Romeo?
NURSE. *[Exasperated]* Romeo, Romeo, wherefore art thou Romeo! She is moonstruck by that calf stripling! *[To audience]* All I hear is -- A-aaah, Romeo, and O-oooooh, Romeo! And Romeo This and Romeo That! Her tongue forever breathes the name of Romeo. E'en when she lies asleep in her as yet -- Heaven Be Praised -- virgin bed -- her lips are constant in their shape of -- *[She makes great play of miming with her lips.]* -- Rom - e - o! *[Turning in direction of JULIET's voice, she yells.]* Jul -- i -- et!!

5

[JULIET enters at the top of the steps. She is in a swoon of love, and looks at her half-uplifted hand as though it were a jewel.]

NURSE. The wench is still in a cloud-spun enchantment of love. That boy will be the death of her yet.

JULIET. You spoke, sweet nurse?

NURSE. Aye! I spoke! For the past ten minutes, I have been speaking, but you have been blind, deaf and dumb to all my exhortations.

JULIET. *[Scarecely heeding her]* He kissed this hand -- this very hand!

NURSE. *[To audience]* She is besotted of love. My Christian duty is plain -- to unbesot her. Juliet, when have I wrongly counselled thee?

JULIET. Counselled, nurse? Wrongly, nurse?

NURSE. She is in a daze of love, and heeds not the common currency of every-day words. Listen, maid. We have been summoned here by certain illustrious names.

JULIET. *[Still dreaming]* Illustrious names? *[Coming rapturously to life]* You cannot mean -- Romeo?

NURSE. *[Tartly]* You are right. I cannot! The illustrious names are all writ here. See for yourself.

JULIET. *[Wanders around the table, facing the audience, reading the small cards at each place.]* Kate the Shrew. Cleopatra . . . . Cleopatra? Oh - Cleopatra! Desdemona. Juliet . . . . me. Lady Mac - Beth. *[Separates the two syllables]* Mac - Beth? Who is she?

NURSE. It is she who has called this Council of Women. For what reason, I know not.

JULIET. But, who is she? A curious sounding name.

NURSE. From a curious sounding country. A country of barbarians, where men sport rainbow-tinted skirts, and make music with a pig's bladder.

JULIET. *[Saucy]* So! Do we not make music with a cat's gut?

NURSE. Do you treat my grey hairs with becoming respect,
madam. I gave suck to you, and will not brook impertinence.

JULIET. No impertinence was intended, sweet nurse, not to
you who gave me my first milky meal. Think you this
Council will be long about? Romeo still waits, and --

NURSE. *[Interrupting]* Let him wait, girl, let him wait.
Heed this first lesson for all our sex: For every hour a man
is kept waiting, the dish he yearns for will triple in value.

JULIET. *[Sighing]* A-aaaah! Romeo triples in value for me
with every passing moment.

NURSE. *[Aside]* She is trapped in a blind alley of love, and
will not look to the exit.

*[DESDEMONA enters in a rush. She pulls up sharply
when she sees them.]*

DESDEMONA. Oh! 'Tis only you, Juliet, and your serving-
wench.

NURSE. Serving wench! That creature wed to a common
soldier -- and black at that -- she calls me serving wench!

DESDEMONA. A common soldier -- my Othello! He is a
prince among men. Black, yes. The sun has kissed his skin
to shining ebony. I am but a pale dove beside his raven
blackness -- but I am his dove.

JULIET. Desdemona meant no insult, nurse. *[To DESDE-
MONA]* She is of an extreme sensitivity, common to her
calling, but a dear sweet soul for all that.

DESDEMONA. I care not for her or her calling. All I am
interested in is this Council -- this meeting -- this -- this ---
Why have we been summoned here?

JULIET. It is a mystery to us, too.

NURSE. All I know is, 'tis only for the likes of us.

DESDEMONA. *[Disdainfully]* The likes of us!

NURSE. Aye, madam! The likes of us! Your fine clothes
may conceit you to think different, but 'neath your silks

and my calico, I warrant we are fashioned after the self-same pattern!

DESDEMONA. *[Almost speechless]* O-oooh! I would Othello could hear you now!

NURSE. I would he could! And I would not be any pale dove to his raven feathers, that I would tell him, too!

DESDEMONA. O-ooh! O-ooh! Where are the words?!

JULIET. *[The peacemaker]* Desdemona! Sweet Desdemona! Nurse -- the likes of us, you said? You mean -- no gentlemen will be present?

NURSE. Aye! No gentlemen. But women galore! Lasses! Dames! Damsels! Maids! Wenches! Mistresses! Wives!

DESDEMONA. A Merry Regiment of Women, indeed!

JULIET. *[Off again]* Wife -- to Romeo!

NURSE. Juliet! Where is thy modesty!

JULIET. Alas, threadbare as a monk's robe! When there is love, where is the need for modesty?

NURSE. *[Shocked]* O-oooooh!

[LADY MACBETH enters in a whirl.]

LADY MAC. A-aaah! Ladies! My most dire apologies for so tardy an arrival. My Lord MacBeth -- he does not merely talk, that man. He would out-tongue a Scottish Chieftain in his cups.

DESDEMONA. Which is hardly surprising, since he is a Scottish Chieftain.

LADY MAC. Ahem! Is all in readiness for our Council? *[Looking at table with cards, etc.]* Aye, well enough. Katherine is yet to come -- and where is Cleopatra?

NURSE. *[Scornfully]* That Egyptian trollop!

LADY MAC. Now now, Nurse! Charity in all things. Where can she be?

NURSE. I could hazard a right good guess!

DESDEMONA. Please! No vulgarity!

JULIET. Cleopatra . . . ? I seem to have heard of a certain . . .

what was his name . . . . a-aah - Antony!

NURSE. *[Pointedly]* That was **one** of the names!

LADY MAC. No tittle-tattle, I beg. We are not here for shrewish gossip. Our business is of a serious nature.

DESDEMONA. If only I might be told what this business is! There is so little time, and my midnight-skinned Othello is impatient for me.

NURSE. *[Shocked]* Was ever a hussy so brazen! *[From off, we hear a MAN's voice calling: Juliet! Juliet! Wherefore Art Thou, Juliet!]*

JULIET. *[Galvanized]* Romeo, Romeo! Wherefore art thou, Romeo!

[She makes swift exit from top of the steps.]

LADY MAC. The younger generation! 'T'was never like this in Scotland. *[Calls after her]* Juliet! We await you!

NURSE. As well speak to that dumb table and expect an answer. Her ears are deaf to all but Romeo's voice.

DESDEMONA. *[Sighing]* How well I understand that.

NURSE. Aye! How well I understand how you understand that!

LADY MAC. Ladies, ladies! I beg you!

DESDEMONA. Ladies? You class that – that peasant -- with me!

NURSE. Peasant! She calls me peasant! I -- who have been wet-nurse to royalty! For that, madam, I might well --

LADY MAC. *[Interposing]* -- Desdemona! Nurse! No quarreling! We must be of one mind and one purpose, else the purpose of this meeting will fail.

[As CLEOPATRA makes a queenly entrance.]

A-aah! Here is Cleopatra. At last!

CLEO. Did I hear allusion to my illustrious self?

NURSE. The conceit of these foreigners would make a

drunken sailor sober.

LADY MAC. I said -- at last! A little matter of time, Cleopatra. It has been said -- Punctuality is the Courtesy of Kings.

CLEO. Then kings can have it and welcome! I am called Queen.

NURSE. Among other things!

LADY MAC. Nurse! Go and summon your charge.

NURSE. H'mph! I'll do my best,
                         E'en though it comes to Romeo's worst!

[NURSE exits.]

CLEO. *[Woman to woman]* Rumor has it that you have a preference for a lord of dusky skin.

DESDEMONA. Preference is a pale and puny word for the passion which burns in me for Othello.

CLEO. And I for Caesar -- *[Hastily recollecting]* -- I mean, Antony.

LADY MAC. Ladies, this is no time for bedroom confidences. Where is Katherine?

CLEO. *[None too pleased]* Do you tell me that Kate the Shrew has been invited?

LADY MAC. Aye. Why should she not be?

CLEO. Because she is what she is well named -- a Shrew.

LADY MAC. When she has a mind to it, she can be gentle.

DESDEMONA. Hah! Gentle as a prancing stallion!

LADY MAC. A **black** stallion!

CLEO. Ho-ho! Such conversation -- and between ladies! 'T'were better suited to a tap-room!

[Enter KATE, a rose not overblown, but definitely blown about, she erupts onto the stage, talking as she enters.]

KATE. Ho! Such a sight to behold! Such a truly sad and pathetic sight! Such a mocking and ridiculous sight! Such a droll and comic sight! Such a --

LADY MAC. *[Stemming flood]* -- this so many adjectival sight -- what is it? Where is it?

KATE. Outside on the moon-swept balcony! A boy with outstretched arms, and from his beardless lips such extravagant outpourings! *[She mimics his speech:]*
"But, soft! What light through yonder window breaks?
It is the east, and Juliet is the sun.
Arise, fair sun, and kill the envious moon!"
[Resuming her own voice] Ha, ha, ha! Never did I hear the like!

DESDEMONA. *[Coldly]* Do you not recognize **love** when you see it?

KATE. Love? Love! Bah! I spit on it!

DESDEMONA. Then, madam, you spit alone.

CLEO. In complete solitude.

KATE. So! For my part, that is no cause for tears.

CLEO. *[To DESDEMONA]* Truly a barren existence – to be deprived of love.

DESDEMONA. An orphan in the wilderness of life.

KATE. Orphan? Deprived of love? Deprived! I am not deprived. I am blessed with the lack of it. I rejoice in the lack of it. I glory in the lack of it!

DESDEMONA. Methinks she doth protest too much.

KATE. Methinks I have heard that line before!

DESDEMONA. Kate the Scold! Kate the Vixen! Kate the Virago! Kate the Fury! Kate the --

KATE. *[Striking her]* – take that! And that! And that!

LADY MAC. *[Separating them]* You act like beggarmaids and bawds! Where is the dignity of womanhood?

KATE. *[Shouting]* Devil take the dignity of womanhood!

DESDEMONA. *[Rearranging costume]* Believe me, ladies, Othello has never seen me in such sad disarray.

KATE. *[Flinging the word at her]* Is he then a Eunich!?

DESDEMONA. *[Furious]* Oh! Would my nails were talontipped to tear out her hell-cat eyes!

KATE. Hell-cat eyes! She calls me hell-cat eyes!

LADY MAC. Ladies, I entreat you! This is no way for the characters of Shakespeare to act. He would disown us.

KATE. I disown him in advance! I disown all men!

CLEO. Oh, to be back in my barge on the Nile.

KATE. *[With sudden change of mood]* Aye! I would feign fancy that. I have heard talk of this barge -- its purple sails and poop of beaten gold, burnished like a throne.

CLEO. A poor thing, but -- mine own!

DESDEMONA. Not -- Antony's?

CLEO. Nay, save when I am on't enthroned. *[She sighs.]* Then, all is his.

KATE. Always, it comes back to love and talk of love! Lord, how I do detest the word! I would be struck dumb ere it passes my lips again.

CLEO. *[To DESDEMONA]* She is all wild wind and screaming tongue -- but when the storm abates, I warrant she will melt like the rest of us!

DESDEMONA. You speak true, Egypt.

CLEO. An' she had been with me and my Antony last night -- *[She sighs]* -- words are too pale to paint so rich a feast. Royal wench, he called me -- royal wench.

DESDEMONA. *[Superior]* Wench? He called you that!

CLEO. But Royal! It made me woman first and majesty after. No man ever called me that before.

KATE. *[Laughing]* Royal wench! As well call me peasant queen!

DESDEMONA. Peasant fits thee like a well-cut glove, but --

KATE. *[Threatening her again]* -- do not say it, woman, do not dare to utter it!

LADY MAC. Enough, enough! Now, the Nurse? Where is she?

CLEO. Shuffling unwanted attendance on her mistress, I doubt not.

KATE. Aye. That Juliana - Julietta -

DESDEMONA. Juliet.

LADY MAC. Then, summon them here.

DESDEMONA. You ask me to act as servant?!

KATE. Faith, an' it were your blackamoor, you would be bellowing soon enough. *[She goes to exit and yells.]* Juliana! Julietta!

CLEO. Juliet!

KATE. *[Shrugging]* What's in a name? A rose by any other, etcetera, etcetera, etcetera!

[Enter NURSE.]

NURSE.   'Tis good to 'scape from lovers' vows.
            On each and every gasping sigh
            Either must I weep or shriek with laughter . . .

CLEO. Poor ancient soul! The hot blood chills with age, and passion's but a cooling memory.

NURSE. Cooling memory, maybe, but 't'were one marriage and one alone that bore witness to my hard-won chastity.

LADY MAC. Ach, woman! You wear your virtue like a rusting medal! Where is Juliet?

NURSE. As always, swearing vows eternal to her Romeo -- with Romeo out-vowing her at every breath.

KATE. *[Scornfully]* Vows eternal! The currency of lovers --
            Today's coinage · Tomorrow's worthless
                        coin.

[JULIET appears on top of the steps.]

JULIET.   Oh! Goodnight, goodnight!
            Parting is such sweet sorrow,
            That I shall say goodnight till it be morrow.
    [CLEO. and DESDEMONA sigh sentimentally as they look at her.]

LADY MAC. *[Breaking spell briskly]* I warrant more will be said here this night than a languishing goodnight. Queen, ladies, maid and hireling, pray be seated.
    [Facing audience, they ALL sit with exception of NURSE.

LADY MACBETH in center. KATE and DESDEMONA find themselves next to each other, so KATE pointedly picks up her card and moves to the other side of LADY MACBETH, JULIET taking her place.]

NURSE. Does no card read my name?

LADY MAC. You have no name. You are but Juliet's Nurse.

NURSE. No name, no name? What say you -- no name -- ?

DESDEMONA. Maybe she is deaf as well as virtuous.

CLEO. Mayhap the one is the cause of the other.

LADY MAC. *[Very much the chairman]* And know you why she has no name? Ladies, can you answer it?

JULIET. Is this a riddle? I cannot fathom riddles.

LADY MAC. No riddle, I swear. All this is part of the business of our meeting. In truth, the whole part.

CLEO. *[Aside]* Business! Council! Meeting! I would rather sit on the needle-point of a pyramid than hark to the cackle of these scratching hens.

KATE. *[Laughing]* Scratching hens! Think you I am broody and about to drop an egg!

DESDEMONA. *[Disgusted]* O-o-oooooh!

CLEO. *[Smothering yawn]* We are waiting.

LADY MAC. In a word – two words: Will Shakespeare.

KATE. *[Scornfully]* Will Shakespeare! That mountebank of the playhouse!

DESDEMONA. Hold thy treacherous tongue, Kate. He is our father.

KATE. Father, father! I would not have him for a father an' he were the one man in the world!

CLEO. *[Sighing]* An' he were the one man in the world, I would not want him for a father.

NURSE. Every word she speaks brands her as a bawd.

LADY MAC. Attention, ladies! To resume. This is a meeting to voice our protest . . . . *[Immediately they ALL break out into a hubbub of voices.]*

VOICES. Protest? Protest? Against whom? Against what? Why, why? *[Etc., etc.]*

LADY MAC. *[Raising a dignified hand]* Silence! Thank you. Ahem! We are all women, are we not?

KATE. God knows I have made protest oft enough about that! I protest! -- Is that our protest?

CLEO. Heaven forbid! I would not be other than a woman while such men as Antony live and have their being!

DESDEMONA. A-aaaaah! Othello! Amen to that!

JULIET. *[Eagerly]* Romeo .... do not forget Romeo!

KATE. *[Scornfully]* Again the Greek chorus chorusing love!

LADY MAC. Ladies, no diversions. Our protest is -- because we are women -- always we are denigrated in Will's plays to the least chief parts.

KATE. Ah! He is a man! He would see well to that! Men!

JULIET. Romeo is a man ....

NURSE. A beardless boy!

LADY MAC. Will Shakespeare is no beardless boy. He knows full well what he is about. He would assume that men are the superior race, and we women the inferior.

KATE. Would I had him here for the half of two minutes! He would be in no doubt who was the superior!

LADY MAC. And because he would have us inferior, so it is with his plays. It is always the men who have the chiefest parts, who command the stage, and the applause of the audience.

KATE. Aye! Truly spoken. That is so, that is so! *[As the OTHERS say nothing, she glares at them.]* Are ye all struck dumb? We await your assent. *[She yells]* Assent!! *[DESDEMONA and CLEO regard each other doubtfully.]*

JULIET. I would not have Romeo have one line less to say.

KATE. Bah! She is too young to know what she is about.

LADY MAC. It was a mistake to invite her.

JULIET. *[Jumping up eagerly]* I may go?

LADY MAC. Juliet! Sit down. *[Glancing wistfully towards exit, she reluctantly seats herself.]* In all his plays, not only do they have the chiefest parts -- almost, they have all the parts.

CLEO. Not all, surely?

DESDEMONA. Surely, not all!

LADY MAC. I will enlighten you. In Hamlet -- you have all heard of Hamlet?

JULIET. Poor Hamlet! He could not make up his mind about Ophelia.

KATE. Hah! He could not make up his mind about anything!

LADY MAC. In Hamlet, a very multitude of men. But -- how many of our own fair sex? *[As they ALL look at one another.]*

KATE. *[Doubtfully]* Ophelia only?

LADY MAC. No -- there is one paltry other. Gertrude -- Queen Gertrude and Ophelia. And two right meager parts they are. While Hamlet! Hamlet scarce leaves the stage!

CLEO. That is but one play. The -- the exception, surely.

LADY MAC. 'Tis a wise child that knows his own father. And it is plain you do not know your paternal Shakespeare.

CLEO. So! Tell us, then.

LADY MAC. Gladly. His play -- The Tempest. Only one of our sex, Miranda. And she is more spirit than woman's flesh and blood -- like that moonstruck Ariel.

DESDEMONA. *[Persuasively]* Yet in MacBeth there is your-self, and . . . . and . . . . *[She falters, not knowing.]*

LADY MAC. And? One more only. Lady MacDuff.

CLEO. Not true! There are the witches -- all three!

LADY MAC. *[Scornfully]* The witches -- all three! As well have them three wizards, three toads, three magpies, for all the womanly attributes they boast! The witches -- all three!

JULIET. *[Dreamily]* If I played a witch, I would make her beautiful.

LADY MAC. Then, you would be confined to the blackness of the wings, girl. Again, there is that piece -- Romeo and Juliet.

JULIET. *[Eagerly]* That play I know.

LADY MAC. Doubtless! And I, too. In it is a category of men as long as a giant's arm, but of women, only four -- and one of them without a name. Nurse to Juliet, she is called. Nurse – to Juliet!

NURSE. *[Sighing]* Aye, that is so. Nurse to Juliet. No name. Not even Bianca. I would feign be called Bianca. Or Emilia . . . or even Maria . . . .

JULIET. *[Running to her]* I would call you Bianca, Nurse!

NURSE. *[Shaking head sadly]* The baptism comes too late, child. Always I will be Nurse now, but . . . *[Brightening]* - I will be Juliet's Nurse. Aye, Juliet's. Never was there a gentler name nor sweeter maid. When posterity reads of Juliet, they will remember -- Nurse to Juliet, too.

JULIET. And Romeo.

NURSE. Aye, child. And thy Romeo.

CLEO. Cleopatra. He named a play after me.

LADY MAC. Did he not name Antony first?

JULIET. I, too, am in the title of the play.

LADY MAC. Aye, but who comes first? It is never Juliet and Romeo, Cleopatra and Antony, Cressida and Troilus! Oh, no! Women and children last!

KATE. My play – The Taming of the Shrew -- I only am in that title. No doubt a lapse of memory by that Stratford glover!

LADY MAC. A right cunning and crafty lapse, Kate. Thou'rt therein named for Taming -- Taming by a **man**!

KATE. 'S'Blood!

NURSE. Aye! Petruchio himself! *[Almost to herself]* I like not the name, but at least it is a name.

LADY MAC. Always it is men. Men, men, men! How that man loved himself!

KATE. Aye! A veritable Narcissus!

LADY MAC. And the abundance of those King plays. King after King after King! Was not the great Elizabeth herself on the throne while he scribbled?

KATE. Aye -- so she was. But where is her play?

LADY MAC. Where, indeed!

DESDEMONA. My play . . . . it is Othello.

LADY MAC. You see -- he does not even mention you -- as he does not mention me -- MacBeth. Not MacBeth and Lady MacBeth. If only I had been named second -- but no! Not even that. Perish the Shakespearian thought!

NURSE. *[Jumping up in excitement]* You! You! You!

DESDEMONA. Now she is in delirium.

NURSE. No delirium, madam. *[To LADY MAC.]* You, too, without a name. Only **his** name. No name of baptism from your literary father. No unique and precious name for you alone. Only -- Lady MacBeth.

LADY MAC. She speaks true. I have no name. Nameless -- anonymous! I live and have my being only through MacBeth – an echo of his name. *[There is a thunderous knocking.]* Nurse! *[NURSE gets up stiffly and makes her laborious way towards entrance.]*

CLEO. Who knocks with such rude violence?

KATE. No woman's hand, I'll warrant!

[NURSE reaches exit when she is swept aside by HENRY V.]

NURSE. Your Majesty -- I beg -- !

HENRY V. No begging, Nurse. Age should never beg of youth, how e'er exalted.

KATE. *[Mocking]* Look who comes here! One of the ubiquitous Henries from a King play -- bursting and belligerent with yet another monologue.

LADY MAC. Aye! I doubt not he will be true to character, and drown us all with yet another spate of words!

HENRY. Ladies, I wish you well, despite your tepid greeting. *[He sniffs delicately]* Do I smell plots and machinations in the air? What's afoot? No mischief against your masters, I trust?

LADY MAC. Masters? We acknowledge no masters!

NURSE. Madam, have a care. He is a King, a Monarch!

LADY MAC. He can be Monarch of a Glen, for all I care!

KATE. Or even Prince of that Wild and Windy Wales!

HENRY.   What! Gentle Ladies,
               This is no welcome for a royal King.
               Your tongues sport blisters,
               And your lips press thin and bloodless as a
                      catscratch.
               Though King, my manhood still persists,
               And women yet have power to charm my royal
                      breast.
LADY MAC. He deigns to notice us!
KATE. Such condescension!
LADY MAC. The conceit of man which passeth all under-
standing!
HENRY.   We would have our women well-favoured,
               Lips softly twinned, appealing outward curves
               Matching the twinned curves beneath;
               Willing, yet not too facile of surrender --
               The chase adds relish to the hunt
               And honey-sweets the victory.
LADY MAC. There speaks the arrogant male!
HENRY. There is an ancient Adam in us all, madam.
CLEO.   Aye! Let us speak true . . . .
               For ever in May-morn bloom
               Our Mother Eve streams restless through the
                      blood.
HENRY.   Egypt speaks with true wisdom of the East.
               Grammercy, Majesty.
KATE. Have a care, Cleo! Thou're not on thy gilded barge
now!
CLEO. I would not offer such strong-armed resistance, an I
were!
NURSE. Mercy on her for a shameless wanton!
LADY MAC. Enough of all this badinage! Will you take your
leave sir? This conference is for ladies only.
HENRY. Ladies only? I am intrigued -- at such intrigue. May
not a mere man enquire as to its purpose?
LADY MAC. Mere man! Hark to that mocking tongue!

KATE. 'S'Blood! Let's inform this strutting majesty! Why hide it secret? No light ever shone beneath a darkening bushel.

JULIET. His Majesty may incline himself to help us.

HENRY. Sweet child . . . . thy Romeo is indeed a fortunate youth.

KATE. *[Shouting]* Tell him -- ere his silver tongue turns all resolution to his serpent will!

HENRY. Would I were Petruchio for one brief hour! It would joy me much to prove who would yield first!

KATE. *[Yelling]* Not I, sirrah, not I!

LADY MAC. *[Banging table]* Order, order! *[As order is restored]* In brief, sire, we here are met to protest against Will Shakespeare.

HENRY. *[Surprised and mildly amused]* Protest -- against our Will -- the author of our being?

LADY MAC. Aye, the author of our being -- who, being a man, did favor his sex with the choicest roles as actors, but denigrated us to parts so mean and paltry, scarce were they worth the learning of his tedious lines!

HENRY. *[Smiling with air of one who has heard it all before]* Faith -- that! Aye, French Kate has shrilled a grumble more than once. *[He shrugs in smiling memory.]* I kissed her protests in a bout of love, and it was soon forgot.

KATE. Lord A'Mighty! If conceit were a dandylion, he'd be a weed-infested cabbage-patch!

CLEO. Kate! Hold thy vixen tongue! It wags too frequent and to no effect.

HENRY. Then let mine wag and to some effect. Why should not dear Will endow us with these Triton parts? Are we not nature's giants in lusty nerve and sinew as well as mental stature? It is we who shape the world and its destiny, who are the architects of history, creators of tomorrow.

LADY MAC. Creators, says this English Harry! Since when have men carried infants? Since when have they given suck to tumbling babes, nursed them through their childish woes,

soothed their peevish whimperings in the long disturbed
nights?

HENRY. Enough, madam, enough! That list of hackneyed
skills might well have been achieved by any animal in whelp.

KATE. *[Livid]* Now -- now he calls us animals!

HENRY. Are we not all animals, firebrand Kate? It is chance
accident of nature that women were thus shaped -- vehicles
to sustain the human race. Brute creation does as much --
all to one purpose -- the furtherance of each individual kind.

LADY MAC. What has all this malicious babble -- of which
there is not one word of truth -- to do with the object of
this meeting?

HENRY. Why -- everything, madam. Will, being an author of
some merit, plucks his characters from life. You surely
must admit to that?

JULIET. *[Eagerly]* Oh, yes, Majesty! *[The REST give
grudging assent, shrugging shoulders, etc.]*

HENRY. So -- of necessity men must play the chiefest roles.
It is man who builds the sprawling cities, raised the myster-
ious pyramids brick by inevitable brick, delves deep into
the black abyss of earth, travels the unquiet seas till he tips
over the horizon. And one day the hand of man shall reach
out even further -- upwards, upwards -- into the infinite sky!

LADY MAC. But --

HENRY. *[Sweeping on]* -- since when have women girded on
cuirass and armour to defend our English shores? While
you lie bedded warm and snug, it is man who is fighting
through the frost-hung night, keeping you safe and shelter-
ed in your several homes. For ours is the glory -- and the
shame! The honor -- and the bubble reputation! The
dignity of rank and gleaming badge -- and the rusting medal
'midst the gross mud of battle! To paraphrase our beloved
Will:

We are such stuff as plays are made on; and our
little life
Is rounded with a pen.

[He makes a sweeping bow.] Farewell, ladies! I would not have the world deprived of the least one of your fair sex!

[Exit HENRY. There is a moment's silence. With the exception of KATE and LADY MAC., they ALL look after him with undisguised admiration.]

KATE. Like all men, he dotes on the sound of his own eloquence!

CLEO. *[Dreamily]* An' I possessed such eloquence, so would I dote.

JULIET. *[Sighing]* I would my Romeo were of a riper age . . .

DESDEMONA. In truth he has a rare charm -- yet I would not change him for my raven Othello.

LADY MAC. *[Bitterly]* Hark to them! It is no cause for wonder we are dubbed the weaker sex.

KATE. A thousand Ayes to that! Frail vessels, all!

DESDEMONA. I, for one, care not if Will Shakespeare has a preference for men actors. How well I understand it!

CLEO. Men have always played the chiefest part in my life. Why should I deny dear Will that privilege in his plays?

LADY MAC. Cleopatra, you are a Queen. Do you bow to a mere man?

CLEO. Already I have told you. I am woman first, and Queen last. Wench Royal! *[Getting up]* This tedious business interests me no longer.

LADY MAC. But, Majesty -- !

CLEO.　　　　No more, I beg! I bid you all farewell.
　　　　　　For as the sun is daily new -- and old --
　　　　　　So is my love still telling what is told.

[Exit CLEOPATRA.]

DESDEMONA. *[Getting up]* Cleo has spoken for me.

LADY MAC. Not possible -- you go -- to Othello?

DESDEMONA.   Aye. To him.
          His beauty shall in these mine eyes be seen,
          And we shall live and keep our love still green.

[Exit DESDEMONA.]

LADY MAC. Traitors to our feminine cause!
KATE. Traitors thrice and thrice again! I hang my head in
     shame for my sex. Othello has but to roll his bullock eyes,
     Antony has but to unbuckle his shield and lift a beckoning
     hand -- and queen and commoner alike -- fly hot-foot to
     their arms. Oh, an' I had two heads, I would hang them
     both in shame! *[A terrific crash offstage.]*
JULIET. *[Alarmed]* Mercy! What can that be!
NURSE. If I mistake not, 'tis the makeshift balcony. Those
     eager lover's feet hath grasshop't once too often!

*[Enter, limping and sucking his finger, a dishevelled
ROMEO.]*

JULIET.   Romeo, Romeo! Thou'rt hurt, my love, my sweet,
          Thou'rt ----
ROMEO. *[Pretending to pretend to make light of it]*
          'Tis nothing --
          But a hair-splinter scratch.
          It will ease out in time.
JULIET. *[Taking his hand]*
          Ease out in time?
          In time it could well poison thee,
          Blacken thy blood with venomous vapours,
          Causing a mortal sickness on thy soul!
     [She eases the splinter from his hand.]
          See! I pluck the intr'ding thorn from thy dear
                         flesh!
          And kiss the raw-edged wound to make it whole.
     [She kisses it.]

ROMEO.   My love!

JULIET.   Art better now? It hurts no more?

ROMEO.   I would my body had a thousand hurts
          Thus to be remedies and healed
          By the love-potion of Juliet's lips!

JULIET.   Gladly would I physician thee!

ROMEO.   And gladly would I take thy 'minstrations.

KATE.   I'faith, the pair of them are past redemption,
          Expiring in love's malady!

LADY MAC. *[Shrugging]*
          An' they once lose the high-pitched tyrant fever,
          This mad delirium will be all forgot.
          The vows of lovers, like the sun-touched ice,
          Soon crack into oblivion.

KATE.   Hah!   The currency of lovers!
                  Today's coinage -
                  Tomorrow's worthless coin.

ROMEO.   Sweet Juliet!
          Now that mine eyes behold thy face most fair,
          My hands can touch thy pearl-tipped, trembling
                              beauty,
          I grow impatient.
          Almost 'tis a feast too rich for man to taste and
                              savour.

JULIET.   Taste, my dear love, and savour deep,
          For never shall ye starve while we two meet.

[They go into a passionate clinch.]

KATE. *[Encircling them]*
          This is a veritable mammoth of a kiss,
          A kiss such would exhaust a lusty Hercules!
          An' I should kiss so long
          I'd have no breath left in my body!

LADY MAC. *[Disgusted]*
          An' I should kiss so long,
          I would not wish breath left in my body.

NURSE. Marry, what would her lady mother say!

[She touches JULIET's arm urgently.]
  Madam! Cherish thy maiden innocence!
  The banns have yet to be announced!
LADY MAC. 'T'were ne'er like this in sober, God-fearing
 Scotland!
ROMEO. Come, Romeo's Juliet, let us on our way,
  For youth is short, and love proclaims its day.

[Exeunt ROMEO and JULIET.]

NURSE. *[Getting up stiffly]*
  The merry-go-round of love goes on and on.
  He knew it all, that knowing Avon Swan.

[Exit NURSE.]

KATE. Juliet and her Romeo! Now her heart dances a mad
 ballet, but time will slow her high kicks to a pedestrian jog-
 trot.
LADY MAC. What to do now? My mission sadly failed, and
 all our hopes splintered on the rock of folly -- and bitt'rest
 pill of all -- female folly!
KATE. Stay! This is defeatist talk! We try again!
LADY MAC. How? In what manner?
KATE. Marry! Summon the others! *[As LADY MAC. looks
 at her, uncomprehendingly.]* Our other sisters! Portia!
 She will be made of sterner stuff. She is half-man already
 in her lawyers's robes. And Viola! Olivia! And Diana!
 There is a host to choose from.
LADY MAC. A host, indeed! You hearten me much, Kate.
 Your presence here has saved our feminine day. No cause
 had better advocate.
KATE. Men! I would denounce them all!
   Challenge each mother's son to do battle
   And grind them into dunghill Dust!

[Enter PETRUCHIO.]

PETRUCHIO.   Battle, Fair Kate! You would do battle . . .?
             Then here's my call to arms --
             And here's my eager battlefield!
[He tries to seize KATE in a rough embrace.]
KATE. *[Yelling and resisting]* Let go, sirrah, let go!
PETRUCHIO. Never!
KATE. Let -- Go!
PETRUCHIO. Save thy hot breath to cool my blazing ardour!
*[She strikes him. He lets her go, and she falls in an ungainly
spread-eagled heap on the floor.]*
          'S'Blood, she wields a monstrous hefty fist --
          Enough to spear a lesser man in two!
KATE. *[Yelling from floor]*
          Thou carrion dog! Thou crawling serpent's belly!
          Thou weed of weeds, thou less than farmyard scum!
PETRUCHIO. *[Looking down at her, smilingly triumphant]*
          Faith, thou art a truly tempting sight!
          I joy the look of ye from this provoking height!
KATE. *[Scrambling to her feet and striking his helping hand]*
    I'll joy the look of ye to see thee prostrate and provoked!
PETRUCHIO.   I'll cart thee to the church, wench, an' I
                  burst my heart in th' doing!
KATE.   I'll see thee buried ten foot churchyard deep!
PETRUCHIO.   I'll see thee marriage vowing 'fore a parying
                  priest!
KATE.   I'll see thy coffin, and ne'er shed a tear!
PETRUCHIO.   I'll see thee simper at our wedding feast!
KATE.   I'll fun'ral thee and shout a cheerful song!
PETRUCHIO. *[Snatching a flower from her corsage or what-
ever.]* She loves me! She loves me not! *[In tones of de-
lighted discovery]* She loves me! Aye, she loves me!
KATE. *[Snatching flower from him and tearing it]* Not! Not!
Not!
PETRUCHIO.   A woman's Nay is often turned to Yea,

And oft' the more she protests,
The more she'll change her say!

KATE. Not I, sirrah, not I!
I'll flee thee to the end of endless time!

PETRUCHIO. Not so, not so . . . .
My feet will ever be more fleet than thine!

KATE. Plague on thy feet, and all the rest of ye!
I'll not have thee to wed, not thro' eternity!

PETRUCHIO. Kate, Kate! Hot blooded and hot headed,
Yet warm of heart beneath that stormy breast.
I would -- O -- how I would --

KATE. *[Breaking in]* -- I would, thou wouldst, he would!
I would you would take off elsewhere,
And ne'er again affront my eyes with sight of
thy barbarian face!

PETRUCHIO. Sweet Kate! Honeyed Kate! Blistering, teeth-
edged, tempestuous Kate! Though your voice speaks you
an irksome, brawling scold, yet your eyes speak me fair!

KATE. Then my eyes deceive you, sirrah!
Naught from my eyes or any part of me
Would ever speak you fair!

*[Offstage, we hear an attractive feminine voice, cooing yet
penetrating.]*

FEMININE VOICE. Pet - ruch - io! Pet - ruch - io!

KATE. *[Jealously]* Who calls?

PETRUCHIO. *[Sighing with gusto]* Lord! Again she follows
in my footsteps! I must away!

KATE. Tarry not on my behalf! She is more than welcome
to thee.

PETRUCHIO. *[Going towards exit]* I come, sweet Margaret!

KATE. Margaret? Margaret!

PETRUCHIO. Aye . . . . Margaret. Like you not the name?
[As KATE shrugs] She is a comely buxom wench,
With all her shapely body shouting the come-hither.
Always she calls: *[Miming feminine voice]* Petruchio!
Petruchio!

[Resuming own voice] An' I let her shout in vain,
    I would not be a man!
[During above speech, KATE has been fussing with her hair, dress, etc.]

KATE. *[Meltingly]* But who should know better than I that thou'rt a man? Have I said aught to the contrary?

PETRUCHIO. *[Meaningly]* Thou has said naught to much.

KATE. Much? What is this 'much' that thou wouldst ask of me? Tell me, Petruchio.

OFFSTAGE VOICE. *[Feminine voice calls again]* Pet--ruch--io!

KATE. *[Yelling, tearing offstage as she does so]* Get thee hence, strumpet! Away with thee!

[Exit KATE, and we hear violent thumps and screams.]

LADY MAC.   So, Petruchio!
        Tho' we're not in Denmark,
        My nose tells me that something rotten is afoot!

PETRUCHIO. *[All innocence]* Rotten, gentle lady? You speak in riddles.

LADY MAC. This riddle is giant plain.
        I know this Margaret wench. She is to wed
            thy servant.
        Thou'st been right busy with thy bribes, a sop
            for Cerberus!

PETRUCHIO. Nay, nay -- not him.
        Say rather, the off'ring's at the foot of Cupid!

[Enter in a vounce, KATE, bedraggled but triumphant.]

PETRUCHIO.   All is well, my Katherine?

KATE.   Aye! For me!
        For her -- that shameless Meg --
        Ha! 'T'will be many a long moon afore she
            follows any man's footsteps!

PETRUCHIO.   My firebrand Kate!

I love thy fearless spirit.

KATE.   Tell me, Petruchio, what is this 'much' thou wouldst demand of me?

[He gives audience a conspiritorial wink, then, with lovers' arms around each other, exeunt KATE and PETRUCHIO. As LADY MACBETH begins her final speech . . . . . . Enter the NURSE, unobstrusively, from R. She holds a long candle snuffer, and, as LADY MACBETH speaks, the NURSE quietly snuffs out the candles on the chandelier, the stage lights gradually dimming as she does so, timing the final candle out to coincide with LADY MACBETH's last line.]

LADY MAC.   Kate, Kate, Kate, Kate!
Treason from thee goes deeper than ten spears!
"There are our sisters -- a host to choose from!"
O mouthing mockery of words!
They split the heavens with deafening impre-
                cations,
Yet actions shout them liars!
Sisters who spurt black venom with their
                tongue,
Yet -- at first brush of beard or rough-hewn lip,
The venom's vanished into honey glow --
The imprecations turned to blessings!

Once more the battle's lost, the Bard has won,
O Sweet Will Shakespeare, would I were a man!

[CURTAIN – THE END]

MUSIC USE NOTE

Licensees are solely responsible for obtaining formal written permission from copyright owners to use copyrighted music in the performance of this play and are strongly cautioned to do so. If no such permission is obtained by the licensee, then the licensee must use only original music that the licensee owns and controls. Licensees are solely responsible and liable for all music clearances and shall indemnify the copyright owners of the play(s) and their licensing agent, Samuel French, against any costs, expenses, losses and liabilities arising from the use of music by licensees. Please contact the appropriate music licensing authority in your territory for the rights to any incidental music.

IMPORTANT BILLING AND CREDIT REQUIREMENTS

If you have obtained performance rights to this title, please refer to your licensing agreement for important billing and credit requirements.